FOR
KT-384-951

TITCHY WITCH AND THE MAGIC PARTY

C016044836

For Beccy
R.I.

To Nichy-noo
K.M.

ORCHARD BOOKS
338 Euston Road, London NW1 3BH
Orchard Books Australia
Level 17/207 Kent Street, Sydney, NWS 2000
First published in Great Britain in 2003
First paperback publication in 2004
This edition published in 2015
ISBN 978 1 40833 785 1
Text © Rose Impey 2003 Illustrations © Katharine McEwen 2003
The rights of Rose Impey to be identified as the author and
Katharine McEwen to be identified as the illustrator of this Work
have been asserted by them in accordance with the
Copyright, Designs and Patents Act, 1988.
A CIP catalogue record for this book is available from the British Library
1 3 5 7 9 10 8 6 4 2
Printed in China
Orchard Books is a division of Hachette Children's Books,
an Hachette UK company
www.hachette.co.uk

TITCHY WITCH AND THE MAGIC PARTY

ROSE IMPEY ★ KATHARINE McEWEN

ORCHARD

Titchy-witch
Victor
Eric
Wendel
Weeny-witch
Witchy-witch
Cat-a-bogus

It was almost Halloween.
Witchy-witch and Wendel were
having a big party.

Titchy-witch wanted a party too. "Of course, my little bewitcher," said Mum. "Cat-a-bogus will do the food."

Titchy-witch wanted all her favourite things.

Mounds of maggot and
marmalade sandwiches,
piles of slug and pickle pizzas,
mountains of frogspawn jelly
and a colossal cake.

Is that all?

Titchy-witch made a list of party games too.

And prizes!

"Big bags of Wiggly Wagglies and Drobble-drops and Squibblies."

"I hope no-one's sick," said Cat-a-bogus.

But then Titchy-witch didn't know who to invite to her party.

Primrose was really prissy.

And Gobby-goblin poked her all the time.

And Wilfy-wolf played tricks on her.

And Clever Jack was the teacher's pet.

"Haven't got any friends," said Titchy-witch.
"Well, a party's a good way to make some," said Wendel.

But when the party arrived,
Titchy-witch didn't think
she was going to enjoy
it very much.

She scowled when Clever Jack won all the Drobble-drops.

She gritted her fangs when Gobby-goblin cheated at Crab-Apple Bobbing.

And when Primrose won at Musical Broomsticks, she was so cross she wiggled her nose...

...and made Primrose's broomstick disappear.

Mum and Dad told her to hand round the food and be a good little witch. But she wasn't.

Suddenly Primrose had a tail.

Clever Jack grew a pair of rabbit's ears.

Gobby-goblin started breathing fire.

And Wilfy-Wolf found he could fly.

Mum and Dad nearly put a stop to it.

But everyone was having such a good time.

"You are clever," said Clever Jack.
"I wish I was a witch, like you,"
said Primrose.

Even Gobby-goblin asked Titchy-witch to come to his cave for tea.

At the end of the party Cat-a-bogus was waiting at the door. He made sure everyone went home the same as they had come.

Well, almost every one.

"Please let me keep it," begged Primrose. "Just till Monday."
"All right," said Titchy-witch.

Primrose gave her a big hug.
"You're my best friend ever,"
she said.

TITCHY WITCH

BY ROSE IMPEY ILLUSTRATED BY KATHARINE McEWEN

Enjoy a little more magic with all the Titchy-witch tales:

- ❑ Titchy-witch and the Birthday Broomstick
- ❑ Titchy-witch and the Disappearing Baby
- ❑ Titchy-witch and the Frog Fiasco
- ❑ Titchy-witch and the Stray Dragon
- ❑ Titchy-witch and the Bully-Boggarts
- ❑ Titchy-witch and the Wobbly Fang
- ❑ Titchy-witch and the Get-Better Spell
- ❑ Titchy-witch and the Magic Party
- ❑ Titchy-witch and the Teacher-Charming Spell
- ❑ Titchy-witch and the Scary Haircut
- ❑ Titchy-witch and the Babysitting Spell
- ❑ Titchy-witch and the Forbidden Forest

Orchard Books are available from all good bookshops, or can be ordered from our website: www.orchardbooks.co.uk
or telephone 01235 827702, or fax 01235 827703.

Prices and availability are subject to change.